IN CONTROL
Ms Wiz?

Other books about Ms Wiz

Ms Wiz Spells Trouble

In Stitches with Ms Wiz

You're Nicked, Ms Wiz

Ms Wiz Goes Live

Ms Wiz Banned!

Power-Crazy Ms Wiz

Ms Wiz Loves Dracula

Ms Wiz and the Dog from Outer Space

Ms Wiz Rocks!

TERENCE BLACKER
IN CONTROL
Ms Wiz?

Illustrated by
TONY ROSS

ANDERSEN PRESS
LONDON

This edition first published in 2010 by
ANDERSEN PRESS LIMITED
20 Vauxhall Bridge Road
London SW1V 2SA
www.andersenpress.co.uk

First published by Piccadilly Press Limited in 1990

British Library Cataloguing in Publication Data available.

ISBN 978 1 84939 152 8

Printed in China

IN CONTROL
Ms Wiz?

CHAPTER ONE
"WHO WAS THAT WOMAN?"

Above Mr Goff's desk at the Latimer Road Library was a sign that read "QUIET, PLEASE!" Today, as usual, it was being ignored.

In the children's corner, a group of five-year-olds were laughing at a story being read to them by their teacher.

By one of the armchairs, a bluebottle was buzzing around the head of an old man who had fallen asleep.

Among the bookshelves, the new assistant librarian was flicking her duster at the books like a charioteer cracking a whip.

At the front desk, Mr Goff was sniffling into his handkerchief.

And, in the reference section, Peter Harris – "Podge" to everyone who knew him – was telling his school friend Jack Beddows some really interesting facts he had just discovered.

"Did you know that in 1955, Phillip Yadzik of Chicago, USA, ate 77 large hamburgers in two hours?"

"Gross," said Jack, who was trying to read a football book.

"Or that the heaviest man in the world came from East Ham, England, and weighed an astonishing 59 stone?"

"Mmm, big," said Jack.

"And that the world's largest jelly—"

"Podge," said Jack, putting down his book. "Did you know that the most annoying person in the entire universe is Podge 'Motormouth'

Harris of London, England, who once had a *Guinness Book of Records* pushed right up his left nostril because he talked about food all the time?"

"All right, all right," said Podge. "I was just trying to improve your general knowledge."

At that moment, the sniffling noise coming from Mr Goff's desk stopped. He took a deep breath and went, "Wah-wah-wah-WAAHHH!"

It was an extraordinary noise for anyone to make and it was particularly strange coming from Mr Goff, who was a timid, polite man. Normally, the only sound he ever made was the occasional "Sssshhh!"

Everybody stared. Mr Goff removed his spectacles and wiped them with a handkerchief. He looked around the library, sniffed a few times and took another deep breath.

"WAAAAHHHHHH!"

"Fire!" said the old man in the armchair, waking up with a start. "Don't panic! I heard the siren! Pensioners out first!"

"Podge," said Jack out of the side of his mouth. "I think the librarian is crying."

"How embarrassing," said Podge.

The teacher who had been reading to the children walked over to the front desk.

"Are you all right, Mr Goff?" she asked.

The librarian sniffed miserably.

"Perhaps it's hay fever," said the old man, who had now realised that the noise which had woken him was not a fire alarm.

Podge and Jack joined the group now standing around the front desk. They felt sorry for Mr Goff but, not being used to grown librarians bursting into tears in the middle of the day, they couldn't think of anything to say.

The new assistant librarian, a young woman with her dark hair in a ponytail, went round to the other side of the desk and put her arm around Mr Goff.

"Cheer up," she said. "It might never happen."

"It already has," said the librarian miserably. He gave her the sheet of paper that he had been reading. "Look at this note from the council."

"*Notice of closure,*" the assistant librarian read out. "*The council gives notice that, as from the end of this month, the Latimer Road Library will be closed—*"

"Oh dear," said the teacher.

"*—and that all the books will be transferred to the nearby St Edward's Road Library—*"

7

"Nearby?" said the old man. "It's too far for me to walk to."

"The library staff will be given jobs in another library. Signed, The Chief Leisure Officer."

"I don't want a job in another library," said Mr Goff, his voice cracking as if he were about to cry again. The teacher put her arm around his shoulders.

"There, there," she said.

"Jack," said Podge, looking closely at the assistant librarian, who was now taking off her nylon cleaning coat. "Does she remind you of someone?"

"Yes, she does," said Jack. "But what on earth is she doing here?"

The assistant librarian briskly peeled off the gloves in which she had been dusting the shelves. Standing

8

there in her purple T-shirt and jeans, she looked quite different.

"It must be her," said Podge. "Who else would wear black nail varnish to work in a library?"

"That's enough talk," said the assistant librarian with her hands on her hips. "It's time for action. The end of the month – that means they'll be closing the library on Friday, unless we can stop them. Jack, Podge – I'll need your help. Now here's what we're going to do..."

Jack and Podge exchanged glances. She knew their names. "Here we go again," said Podge with a smile.

A few minutes later, the assistant librarian gathered up her belongings and strode out of the library, saying she had some spells to prepare.

"Spells?" said the teacher after she had left. "What's going on?"

"Yes, who *was* that woman in the purple T-shirt?" asked Mr Goff.

"That was Ms Wiz," said Podge.

"If anyone can save the library," said Jack, "Ms Wiz can. She has magic on her side."

"Good old Ms Wiz," said Mr Goff. He didn't seem convinced.

"Dad," said Podge that evening, as the Harris family ate dinner. "Is it true that the council wants to close the library?"

"It is," said Mr Harris, who was a councillor. "There are too many libraries in this area. We're selling it to make flats." He stabbed a sausage

with his fork. "Very nice flats they'll be too."

"What about the people who use the library?" asked Podge. "They matter too."

"Don't be cheeky to your father," said Mrs Harris.

"It's true," Podge insisted. "People need that library. And—" Podge lowered his voice, "—Ms Wiz is going to save it."

"Did you say Wiz? Is that Wiz woman getting involved?" Mr Harris looked worried. He remembered last term at St Barnabas when an owl taught maths, a school inspector found a rat in his trousers and two of the teachers were turned into geese. "That woman spells trouble."

"*Someone*'s got to save our books for us," said Podge.

Mr Harris dipped his sausage into some tomato sauce.

"Remember this, son," he said solemnly. "Books are books – and business is business. And never the twain shall meet. Am I right, Mum?"

"You certainly are, Dad," said Mrs Harris.

CHAPTER TWO
"IS THIS A LIBRARY OR A ZOO?"

That Friday afternoon, Jack and Podge met in the park and set off for Latimer Road Library. Jack brought his skateboard, because he took his skateboard everywhere, and Podge brought a large box of sandwiches, just in case saving the library carried on over tea-time.

But when they arrived at Latimer Road, they received a shock. The library was closed and Mr Goff was sitting on the steps outside, looking miserable.

"They've locked it up," he said. "My own library and I can't get in."

"That's strange," said Jack. "It

wasn't meant to be closed until tonight."

"Maybe the Chief Leisure Officer heard that your Ms Wiz had magic on her mind," said Mr Goff.

"But how?" Jack was puzzled. "It was meant to be a secret. No one would be stupid enough to blab to someone on the council, would they?"

"Well . . . " Podge was looking as if he wished he were somewhere else.

"Oh no," said Jack. "You didn't mention it to your father, did you?"

"You see—"

"Podge," said Jack wearily. "You are a complete and utter nerdbrain."

"Perhaps Ms Wiz will know what to do," said Podge weakly.

Mr Goff sniffed. "If she turns up."

"She'll be here soon," said Jack.

"She'll probably fly in on her vacuum cleaner."

"Or just appear out of thin air," said Podge.

At that moment, the number 22 bus drew up in front of the library. Ms Wiz stepped out, carrying a plastic bag.

"Huh," said Mr Goff. "Some witch."

Ms Wiz was against giving up and

going home (Mr Goff's suggestion), or smashing the door down (Jack's suggestion), or discussing the whole thing over a few sandwiches and cakes (Podge's suggestion).

"The people from the council will be here soon," she said. "After all, no one has told Mr Goff what's going to happen to him."

"What do we do when they get here?" asked Mr Goff.

"We magic 'em," said Podge with a grin.

"Yeah," said Jack. "Ms Wiz will use Hecate, the china cat with flashing eyes, Archie the owl and Herbert the magic rat."

"Oh, whoops!" Ms Wiz clapped a hand to her forehead. "I left them all at home."

Mr Goff, Jack and Podge looked at her in amazement.

"All right," she said with a shrug. "Nobody's perfect."

"Well, what *have* you got?" asked Jack, beginning to wonder whether Ms Wiz was a bit less magic than she used to be.

Ms Wiz looked inside her plastic

bag and eventually brought out a small bottle the size of a pepperpot.

"I've got some Fish Powder," she said.

"Great," said Podge. "We can sprinkle it on my sandwiches. Fish and peanut butter. Yummy."

"And how," asked Mr Goff, "is fish powder going to save a library?"

"This is special Fish Powder," said Ms Wiz. "All we need are some books." She walked briskly towards the library door. "Ah," she said, suddenly remembering that it was locked.

"It's not your day, is it?" said Mr Goff.

Ms Wiz ignored him. "Jack," she said, "have you got any books on you?"

"Nothing much," muttered Jack. "Just a few Beatrix Potters."

"Beatrix Potter?" Podge started to laugh. "Beatrix *Potter*?"

Jack blushed. "They were for my sister," he said.

"Oh no," said Mr Goff, as a car drew up. "Here comes Mrs Prescott, the Chief Leisure Officer."

"Quick!" shouted Ms Wiz. "Give me those books."

Jack pulled a number of small books from his jacket pocket. Ms Wiz laid them on the ground, as the Chief Leisure Officer approached.

"If you close this library down," Ms Wiz called out, reaching for her bottle of Fish Powder, "I shall not be answerable for the consequences."

"This is no longer a library," said

Mrs Prescott. "It's merely a room with books in it. We shall soon remove the books so that it can be converted into flats."

"I warned you," said Ms Wiz, opening the Beatrix Potter books and sprinkling Fish Powder on their pages. There was a slight humming sound, which could be heard above the noise of the traffic on Latimer Road. Then, one by one, a succession of small animals, wearing waistcoats and pinafores, came to life and hopped out of the pages of the books and on to the pavement.

Soon Pigling Bland, the Fierce Bad Rabbit, Jemima Puddle-Duck, Peter Rabbit and several Flopsy Bunnies were hopping, waddling and scurrying about in front of the library.

"Wicked, Ms Wiz," said Jack.

"What's going on?" said Mrs Prescott. "Is this a library or a zoo?"

"This Fish Powder," said Ms Wiz, "can bring any character in a book to life." Jemima Puddle-Duck was wandering off, causing quite a stir outside the newsagent. "We can bring

total confusion to this area unless you leave us our library."

"Fish Powder?" said Mrs Prescott, stepping carefully over the Fierce Bad Rabbit.

"Right," said Ms Wiz. "FISH stands for Freeing Illustrated Storybook Heroes. It's a magic potion."

Podge and Jack gave a cheer.

Ms Wiz held up her hand. "If you don't leave this library alone, I'll release more characters. I can bring this road to a standstill."

"You won't get away with this," said Mrs Prescott, backing towards her car and nearly falling over a Flopsy Bunny in the process. "We'll be back."

She drove off quickly.

"Now," said Ms Wiz. "Let's get these animals under control."

Just then, there was a squeal of brakes from the road behind them.

"Oh no," said Podge. "That's the number 66 bus. I don't think the driver saw one of our animals."

"It's Peter Rabbit!" gasped Jack.

"Peter Rabbit? Under a bus?" Mr Goff had gone pale. "But this could change the whole shape of children's literature."

"It's certainly changed the shape of Peter Rabbit," said Podge, looking into the road.

"He was my favourite," wailed Jack.

"Don't worry," said Ms Wiz. "The Fish Powder will sort him out." She took a deep breath, sprinkled some powder on the pages of *The Tale of Peter Rabbit* and shouted, "HSIF REDWOP!"

The shape in the middle of the road disappeared. Jack looked inside his book.

"Phew!" he said. "Peter's back."

"I thought those books were for your sister," said Podge.

"Never mind that," said Ms Wiz. "We're not going to be able to change

the council's mind with a few Flopsy
Bunnies. What other books have you
got?"

Podge reached inside his lunchbox.
"How about this?" he said.

CHAPTER THREE
"WHERE EXACTLY DID YOU MEET HIM, PETER?"

Mr and Mrs Harris were watching television. This was one of their favourite ways of passing the time, and Mr Harris even used to sneak home on Friday afternoons to watch *The Avenue*, the soap opera he liked most of all.

"That Maylene's heading for trouble," he said to Mrs Harris, as he sipped his tea, waiting for *The Avenue* to begin. "She shouldn't be going out with that dentist when she's already engaged to the schoolteacher."

"No," said Mrs Harris. "Not after what happened at the barbecue."

"Where's the boy?"

For a moment, Mrs Harris thought her husband was still talking about the dentist. Then she realised he meant Peter, their son.

"Down at the library," she said. "Nose in a book as usual."

"Books!" said Podge's father. "Who needs books? When I was his age, I didn't go filling my head with things from books. It never did me any harm. Turn the telly up, Mum."

Mrs Harris turned up the volume on the television.

"Anyway," shouted Mr Harris. "We closed that library today."

"And now—" said the television announcer, "—it's time to visit *The Avenue*."

The front doorbell rang.

"That'll be Peter," said Mr Harris. He got up, grumbling. "If the bell goes at an awkward time when everyone's busy—" he opened the front door, "—it's always . . . er, good afternoon."

There, on the doorstep, was the fattest man Mr Harris had ever seen. He was wearing Bermuda shorts and a baseball cap.

"Can I help you?" asked Mr Harris nervously.

The man pointed to his mouth.

"Hi, dad," said Podge, jumping out from behind the giant. "This is my friend Phillip Yadzik of Chicago, USA."

Mr Harris smiled. "Howdeedodee, Phillip," he said.

"He's rather hungry," said Podge. "He's been in *The Guinness Book of Records* for the last few years."

"Well, he would be," said Mr Harris, looking puzzled.

Yadzik squeezed his way through the front door. Once inside the house, he sniffed the air like a dog at dinner-time.

"Would you like to watch *The Avenue*?" asked Mr Harris weakly. "It's just started."

"I think," said Podge, "he'd rather have a bite to eat."

Yadzik pushed his way past Mr Harris and made for the kitchen. He opened the fridge and gulped down three chicken pies, two dozen sausages and a family box of chips, complete with plastic wrapping.

"Is that Peter with one of his friends?" Mrs Harris called out from next door.

"That's right, Mum," said Podge.

Yadzik was just swallowing a large white loaf of bread, when Podge's mother came out to meet him.

"Oh!" she said. Trying to look normal when a giant is eating his way through your kitchen isn't easy, but somehow Mrs Harris remembered her manners. "What a big boy you are," she said. "Do you go to Peter's school?"

"He doesn't talk," said Podge. "Apparently characters freed from books can't talk. The words belong to their authors."

"I see," said Mrs Harris, who didn't see at all. "Where exactly did you meet him, Peter?"

"In the Food and Gluttony section of *The Guinness Book of Records*. Back in 1955, he ate 77 large hamburgers in two hours. In 1957, he got through 101 bananas in fifteen minutes. But he hasn't eaten for several years, so those records are probably about to be broken."

"Our Sunday lunch," squealed Mrs Harris, as Yadzik found a chicken in the freezer and, with a great crunching noise, sank his teeth into it.

"I don't think he can wait until Sunday," said Podge.

"He's going to eat us out of house and home," said Mr Harris. "Tell him to go away, Peter – please."

"Oh dear," said Podge. "He's going into the front room. I wonder what he'll eat there."

Yadzik sat down heavily on the sofa, breaking all its legs. He casually reached for a cushion and started eating at it.

"He may eat you out of house and home," said Podge casually. "But he'll probably eat the house and home first."

"What are we going to do?" said Mr Harris. Podge had never seen his father look so helpless before.

"The thing is," he answered, as Yadzik tore down a curtain and began chewing one end. "Phillip used to be just a picture in a book. That was his home."

"Yeees?" said Mr Harris, looking puzzled.

"And now someone is closing down the library, where his book was kept. It's the Latimer Road Library."

"Go on," said Mr Harris suspiciously.

"So if someone could just *open* the library," Podge continued, "I'm sure Phillip would be happy to go home. In fact, Ms Wiz just has to sprinkle some powder on his pages and say some funny words and he'll be back in the book, just another weird record."

"Ms Wiz!" said Mr Harris. "I might have known that she'd be involved."

There was a cracking noise as Yadzik crushed a table and started picking at the legs like a smaller person might eat chips.

"I'll ring Mrs Prescott," said Mr Harris, picking up the phone and dialling. "Try and distract him with the television, Mum."

"I wouldn't do that," said Podge.

"Hullo," said Mr Harris into the telephone. "Is that Mrs Prescott, the Chief Leisure Officer? This is Councillor Cuthbert Harris. I want you to open the Latimer Road Library. Yes, this afternoon. It's an emergency."

"Now, Phillip," Mrs Harris was saying. "How about a bit of television?"

"I really don't think that's a good idea," said Podge.

The giant looked at Mrs Harris for a moment. Then his eyes shifted to the television and he smiled.

"No, I'm not drunk," Mr Harris was shouting into the phone. "This Ms Wiz is releasing characters from books. They're everywhere! Hullo? Mrs Prescott? Are you there?"

Yadzik walked over to the television, took out the plug and picked it up with a hungry grunt. He licked his lips.

"Not the television!" screamed Mr Harris, dropping the phone. "You can eat anything but that! NOOOOOOOO!"

CHAPTER FOUR
"PWOBLEM?"

"Um…"

Mr Goff had never been a very brave man. In fact, he was extremely nervous. That was why he had become a librarian. Books were easier to deal with than people. They didn't answer back, or make a noise, or call you names behind your back.

"Um, excuse me…"

That is, until Ms Wiz came along with her Fish Powder. It was all very well saving the library by Freeing Illustrated Storybook Heroes, but once people from books started walking about the place, living their own lives, where would it all end?

"Um, excuse me, I say…"

In trouble. That's where it would
end. Mr Goff tried to imagine what
Latimer Road Library would be like, if
this Fish Powder was being scattered
about. Ms Wiz had said that they
couldn't talk when they were outside
the pages of their books, but what
would happen if someone brought *The
History of the Second World War* to life?

Or *Great Whales of the World*? Or – a terrible thought occurred to him – the rude pictures in some of the Sunday papers? It would cause a riot.

"Um, excuse me, I say, would you mind listening . . . ?"

Ms Wiz, Jack and Podge continued to ignore Mr Goff as, standing outside the library, they discussed what to do next.

"SSSSHHHH!"

At last, they all turned round and noticed that the librarian was trying to say something.

"It seems to me," said Mr Goff, "that this is all getting a bit out of control."

"Not really," said Podge. "Peter Rabbit's back in his book. Ms Wiz returned Phillip to Food and Gluttony by sprinkling Fish Powder on his lines and saying 'HSIF REDWOP' before he ate my house. Shame about the television, though."

"Don't you want to save your library?" asked Jack.

"Of course, I do," said Mr Goff. "But are squashed rabbits and hamburger-crazed Americans really going to help us? Mrs Prescott will simply call the police and that will be that."

"I suppose you're right," said Ms Wiz.

"We need to change Mrs Prescott's mind somehow," said Mr Goff.

"I don't know how," said Ms Wiz. "The library's closed and we haven't got any more books to bring to life."

"Unless—" Mr Goff looked more embarrassed than ever as he reached into his briefcase "—you can use this."

He gave a picture book to Ms Wiz.

"Well done, Mr Goff," she said smiling.

"I was always a bit of a fan of their majesties," he said.

Podge looked at the book.

"I don't get it," he said. "How on earth can *The Bumper Book of Royal Weddings* help us?"

*

When Caroline Smith received a telephone call from her friend Jack, asking for her help, she wasn't a bit surprised.

"Not homework again?" she said.

"We need someone who can do voices," said Jack. "You're the best actress I know. See you at the Town Hall in ten minutes."

"Hang on," said Caroline. "Who's we?"

"Me, Podge – and Ms Wiz."

Caroline gave a little whoop of delight. "I'll be there," she said.

It had been a very normal day for Mrs Prescott, the Chief Leisure Officer. The only interesting thing to happen was a

rather odd call from Cuthbert Harris –
something about the Latimer Road
Library and his television being eaten
– which she had ignored. Cuthbert
sometimes enjoyed a drink or three at
lunchtime. It was probably his idea of
a joke.

There was a knock at the door.

"Come in," said Mrs Prescott.

"I...but...if...sir...help..." It was
her secretary, Mrs Simpson, who
seemed to be having trouble speaking.

"What on *earth* is the matter, Mrs
Simpson?"

"Wheah is the Chief Lejaah
Orficer?" said a loud voice from next
door. "I *demaaaand* to see her!"

The door burst open to reveal the
most unusual visitors Mrs Prescott
had ever received.

"It's their Royal Highnesses," said Mrs Simpson, recovering her voice at last. "A famous prince and princess from Buckingham Palace. They're making a surprise visit to the Town Hall."

"We're gaying walkabout, aaahn't we, deah?" said the voice coming from the princess.

"Don't overdo the accent," Jack whispered to Caroline as they stood, with Podge, Ms Wiz and Mr Goff, behind the royal couple. It was lucky, he thought, that the princess was in her wedding dress and wore a veil over her face. No one could see that her mouth wasn't moving with Caroline's words.

"Are you the Chief Lejaah Orficer?"

"Yes, ma'am." Mrs Prescott was

hurriedly tidying the papers on her desk, while trying to curtsey at the same time. "At your service, ma'am."

The prince, smiling his royal smile, shook her hand.

"Tell meah, may good womaaan," continued Caroline in her princess voice. "How is may favouwite libway, the Latimaaah Woad Libway? Ay *love* weading."

Mrs Prescott winced. "It's c-c-c-closed," she said eventually.

"AY BIG YOUR PAAAHDON?"

"We...I've just closed it down, ma'am."

"May favouwite libway? I wed may vair farst book theah."

Mrs Prescott looked confused.

"I think," said Jack helpfully, "that Her Royal Highness is saying that she read her very first book there."

"Yah," said Caroline.

"Did you, ma'am?" Mrs Prescott was unable to hide her surprise. Somehow the princess didn't look as if she came from the Latimer Road area.

"Ay *demaaaand* that you aypen it. This vair afternoon."

Mrs Prescott gulped.

"We can't aypen – I mean open it," she said. "We've only just closed it. It would be a problem."

"PWOBLEM?" Caroline's voice hit a new high note. "Well, if you can't aypen it, we jolly well shall. Shaaan't we, Pwincey?"

The prince was still smiling his royal smile and shaking hands with everyone. He now stood where

49

Caroline was crouched behind the
princess. He smiled and held out his
hand.

"Leave off, prince," muttered Podge.
"I think she's a bit busy at present."

"Ay'm gaying theah wight now,"
said Caroline. "Ay maight even
mention you in may speech when ay
aypen the libway."

"Speech?" said Jack under his
breath. "I don't believe it."

"Thank you, ma'am." Mrs Prescott

gave a little bob of the head.

"So the Latimah Woad Libway will be aypen again, awight? And stay aypen, OK?"

"Yes, Your Royal Highness," said Mrs Prescott.

"Yeah!" said Jack, rather too loudly.

Mrs Prescott looked up sharply.

"Sorry, ma'am, did you say something?"

"Yah," said Caroline quickly. "OK, yah."

"Ma'am," said Mrs Prescott, blushing. "May I ask Your Royal Highness why you appear to be wearing your wedding dress."

There was a moment's pause.

"Because ... Ectually ... " Caroline was thinking fast. "Because it's may anniverseway. So theah!"

And with that, the royal couple, followed by Caroline, Jack, Podge, Mr Goff and Ms Wiz, swept out of the room.

CHAPTER FIVE
"FRANKENSTEIN COMES TO LATIMER ROAD"

It took quite a long time for the royal party to walk from the Town Hall to Latimer Road because the prince insisted on shaking hands with everyone they met.

"May wedding dwess is getting dusty," said Caroline at one point. "Could you be bwidesmaid and pick it up for me, Podge?"

"You must be joking," said Podge. "Anyway what are you going to say in your speech?"

Caroline laughed. "Ay'll think of something," she said.

A few steps behind them, Mr Goff

was walking with Ms Wiz.

"I can't help noticing," he said, "that you don't seem to be your normal happy self."

Ms Wiz sighed. "You were right, Mr Goff," she said. "It's not my day."

"But why not? The library's going to be re-opened."

"If I tell you something, will you promise not to panic?"

Mr Goff nodded.

"I've lost the Fish Powder. I think someone's taken it."

"Oh dear." Mr Goff started panicking. For some reason, he started thinking about the Second World War. Great Whales of the World. The rude pictures in the Sunday papers. "Oh *dear*!" he said.

By the time the royal couple had

reached Latimer Road, there was quite a crowd following them. Waiting for them at the library was Mrs Prescott, who had driven there as quickly as possible and hung a pink ribbon across the doorway.

"Your Highnesses *walked*?" she said with disbelief in her voice.

Caroline crouched down behind the princess once more.

"We laik to meet the common people," she said loudly.

"Common?" said Jack. "That's nice."

Mrs Prescott gave the princess a pair of scissors.

"If you would be so kind as to cut the ribbon, Your Highness," she said, "we can then open the library."

The princess took the scissors. Behind her, Caroline shouted, "Thenks

to the efforts of your soopah Chief Lejaah Orficer Mrs Prescott, and to your divaine libwawian Mr Goff, not to mention the absolutely spiffing Ms Wiz, ay can declare this libway well and twuly aypen!"

Everyone cheered as the princess cut the ribbon and, closely followed by her prince and Caroline, walked into the library.

Soon the place was as busy as ever. The princess sat down with a group of five-year-olds who were being read a story. The prince shook hands with the old man who was settling back into his favourite armchair.

"Ms Wiz," said Podge. "I think it's Fish Powder time. If you don't return the prince and princess to their book soon, Mrs Prescott's going to get suspicious. Caroline can't keep that voice up much longer."

"Now where *is* that Fish Powder?" said Ms Wiz, rummaging in her plastic bag. "It could really be most embarrassing if it fell into the wrong hands."

Just then a woman fainted at the far end of the library. Standing next to her, looking slightly confused, was a ghost.

"Where has Jack got to?" Ms Wiz asked suddenly.

Podge shrugged. "I think I saw him in the Horror and Ghost section," he said.

"And where's that?"

"Behind where that monster with three heads has just appeared out of thin air."

"*Oh no*!" said Ms Wiz.

Soon the library was in total confusion, with spirits, zombies, werewolves and vampires wandering in and out of the shelves. There were screams of alarm as men, women and children stampeded towards the door. Even the prince and princess looked rather surprised.

"Wow," said Podge. "Frankenstein comes to Latimer Road."

"It's all right," Ms Wiz was shouting. "They can't harm you. They're not real, I promise!"

But no one listened to her.

"Sorreee," said Jack, ambling up to her with the bottle of Fish Powder in his hand. "I just wanted to see if it worked."

Without a word, Ms Wiz took the

bottle and sprinkled powder over the pages Jack had opened.

"HSIF REDWOP!" she shouted. "HSIF REDWOP!"

Gradually, the library was cleared as the demons returned to the books from which they had come.

"I've seen everything now," said Mrs Prescott, who had turned quite white. "A royal visit, then Frankenstein in Latimer Road. I'm glad I don't work here."

"So you won't close us again?" asked Mr Goff.

"Certainly not," said Mrs Prescott, backing out of the door. "This is your library, Mr Goff – and you're welcome to it. Goodbye."

Mr Goff turned to Ms Wiz. "Could I have my *Bumper Book of Royal Weddings* back now?" he asked.

"Of course," said Ms Wiz. "Let me just put the royal couple back." She sprinkled some Fish Powder on to the book and said, "HSIF REDWOP."

The prince and princess started to fade. The last Jack, Podge and Caroline saw of them was a royal smile.

"What a charming couple," said Ms Wiz, giving Mr Goff back his book. "Now, I'd better be off myself."

"Can't you stay?" said Mr Goff.

"The library won't be the same without you."

"Of course it will," said Ms Wiz. "You're the best librarian I've ever met."

Mr Goff blushed.

"Anyway," said Caroline. "Ms Wiz always comes back. She goes wherever magic's needed."

"That's right, Caroline," said Ms Wiz. "Cheerio, everyone."

She held the bottle of Fish Powder high in the air and tapped some out on to her head. "HSIF REDWOP," she said. She smiled, gave a little wave – and faded away.

For the first time in Mr Goff's memory, there was complete silence in the library.

"Whaaaaat?" said Podge eventually. "That means that Ms Wiz is a character in a story."

There was another silence.

"And if she comes from a book," said Caroline, "then where does that leave us?"

"Don't even *think* about it," said Jack.

Sophie and the Albino Camel

STEPHEN DAVIES

'Never mess with the Sahara Desert!'

That's what Sophie's dad is always telling her. But when Sophie meets Gidaado the Fourth and his fine albino camel, the offer of a camel ride is just too good to resist.

It turns out that the Sahara is more dangerous than Sophie could ever have imagined. There are snakes. There are djinns. There are sandstorms. And most terrifying of all there is Moussa ag Litni – a murderous Tuareg bandit intent on stealing camels.

'Pure adventure story . . . An exceptional short novel.' *TES*

9781842705513 £4.99

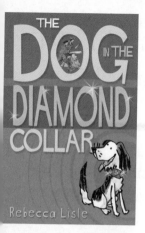

JOE, LAURIE and THEO STORIES

by REBECCA LISLE

with illustrations by TIM ARCHBOLD

Theo has a dog with a very special collar, and the two of them find gnome burglars, a boy lost in a magic box and a boy in a bear pit – all with a great deal of help from older brothers Joe and Laurie, naturally!

All £4.99

The Dog in the Diamond Collar
ISBN: 9781842703663

The Boy in the Big Black Box
ISBN: 9781842706817

The Gnome with the Knobbly Knees
ISBN: 9781842708897

Bobby and Charlton
stories by Sophie Smiley

with illustrations by
MICHAEL FOREMAN

Charlie's family are all football-mad. They always work as a team, whether they have too much snow, a fear of dogs, or are looking for a pirate adventure. And the best player of all is Bobby, who saves all the goals.

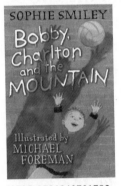

ISBN: 9781842701782

ISBN: 9781842704202

ISBN: 9781842706848

ISBN: 9781842708828

ISBN: 9781842708835

ISBN: 978184939053

All £4.99

DAMIAN DROOTH
SUPERSLEUTH

by Barbara Mitchelhill
with illustrations by Tony Ross

Detective work is Damian's thing, and he does solve all his cases, although he gets into an awful lot of trouble on the way! Read all the books and see how.

All £3.99

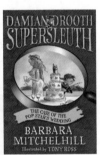

...pearing Daughter
: 9781842705605

Popstar's Wedding
ISBN: 9781842705612

...to be a Detective
: 9781842705971

Spycatcher
ISBN: 9781842705674

Serious Graffiti
ISBN: 9781842706503

...Snatchers
I: 9781842706497

Under Cover
ISBN: 9781842708255

Gruesome Ghosts
ISBN: 9781842708262

Football Forgery
ISBN: 9781849390354

AGENT Amelia

MICHAEL BROAD

Amelia Kidd is a secret agent, and her mission is to save the world. In fact, she's saved it loads of times from criminal masterminds. Read her secret case files, and find out all about it – available three in one book.

Ghost Diamond!
ISBN 9781842706626

Zombie Cows!
ISBN 9781842706633

All £4.99

Hypno Hounds!
ISBN 9781842708163

Spooky Ballet!
ISBN 9781842708170